WHO

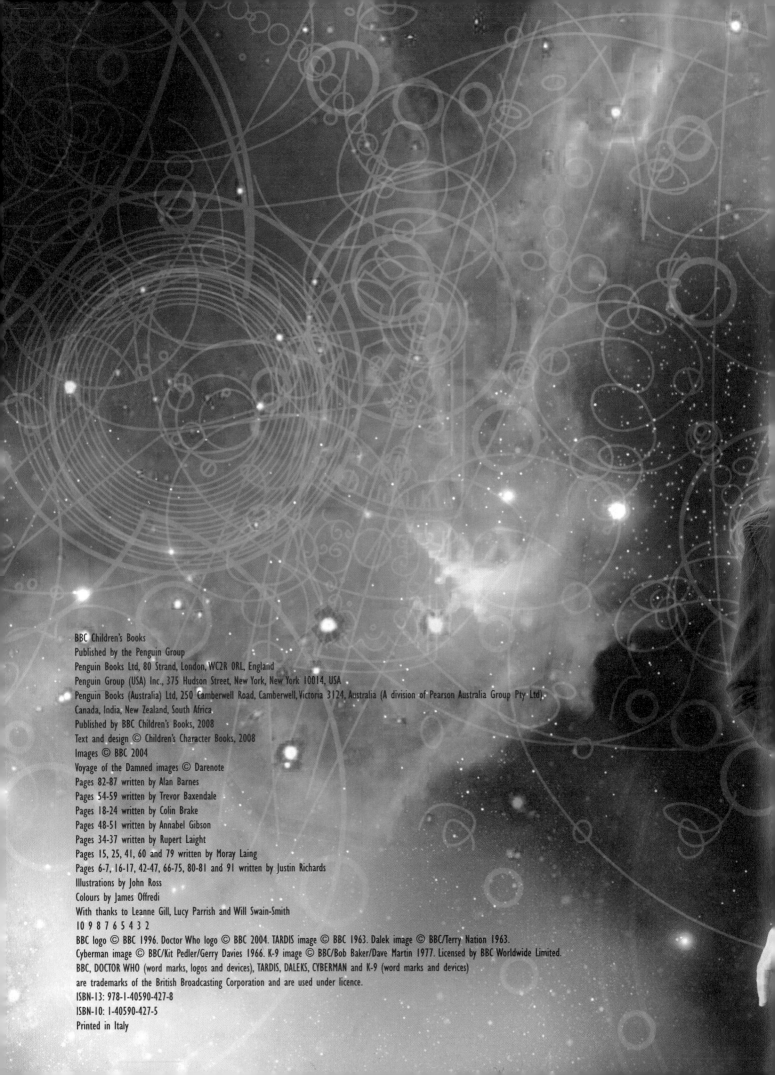

BBC Children's Books
Published by the Penguin Group
Penguin Books Ltd, 80 Strand, London, WC2R 0RL, England
Penguin Group (USA) Inc., 375 Hudson Street, New York, New York 10014, USA
Penguin Books (Australia) Ltd, 250 Camberwell Road, Camberwell, Victoria 3124, Australia (A division of Pearson Australia Group Pty Ltd)
Canada, India, New Zealand, South Africa.
Published by BBC Children's Books, 2008
Text and design © Children's Character Books, 2008
Images © BBC 2004
Voyage of the Damned images © Darenote
Pages 82-87 written by Alan Barnes
Pages 54-59 written by Trevor Baxendale
Pages 18-24 written by Colin Brake
Pages 48-51 written by Annabel Gibson
Pages 34-37 written by Rupert Laight
Pages 15, 25, 41, 60 and 79 written by Moray Laing
Pages 6-7, 16-17, 42-47, 66-75, 80-81 and 91 written by Justin Richards
Illustrations by John Ross
Colours by James Offredi
With thanks to Leanne Gill, Lucy Parrish and Will Swain-Smith
10 9 8 7 6 5 4 3 2
ISBN-13: 978-1-40590-427-8
ISBN-10: 1-40590-427-5
Printed in Italy

# Contents

# The Adventure Continues

## The Doctor went through a lot in his 2007 series of adventures.

He discovered he was not alone in the Universe — that another Time Lord had survived the Great Time War against the Daleks. Then he discovered that the survivor was none other than his fiercest opponent — and childhood friend — the Master.

## Moving On

The Doctor found a new friend in Martha Jones. They hit it off almost at once, trapped together in a hospital transported to the Moon, hiding from Judoon troopers and hunting down a blood-sucking alien Plasmavore. Throughout their adventures together, the Doctor and Martha grew ever closer. Then, after defeating the Master, Martha left. She decided to stay behind on Earth and carry on her life there rather than continue to travel with the Doctor in his amazing TARDIS.

In Cardiff, the Doctor met up again with his friend Captain Jack Harkness. In fact, the Doctor tried to get away before Jack found him — he knows there's something 'wrong' with Jack. He's a man who should be dead. He was brought back to life by Rose Tyler when she was possessed by the energy of the Time Vortex itself. And now, Jack can't die.

Having helped defeat the Master and put history back on its proper course, Jack too left the Doctor — returning to his work at Torchwood and his friends and colleagues there. But not before he sprung one last surprise on the Doctor and Martha. Could he really be the age-old Face of Boe? If he is, then it would explain how the Face of Boe knew the Master had survived — and how he was able to provide such a relevant clue: 'You are not alone'. The initials spell out the name of the Master's 'human' form: Professor Yana.

In New York in the 1930s, the Doctor found the Cult of Skaro — weakened and desperate to survive. And he let one Dalek escape again. The Doctor knows that just one Dalek is enough to threaten the whole Universe...

He has a lot of unfinished business.

# Donna Noble

Donna Noble also has some unfinished business. She turned down the Doctor's offer to travel with him in the TARDIS after their encounter with the Empress of the Racnoss. It turns out she's regretted that decision ever since. Now she's doing her own 'Doctor stuff' – investigating the sinister Adipose Corporation.

And so is the Doctor.

Of course, it's only a matter of time before they meet. This time, Donna's not turning down the Doctor's offer. It's a good choice. Donna gets to see ancient Pompeii – though she's frustrated not to be able to save more of the people from the eruption of Mount Vesuvius. She visits the Ood-Sphere, and helps free the Ood from their slavery. And that's just the start of her amazing adventures with the incredible Doctor...

## New Friends

Donna also meets Martha. She's helping UNIT when the Doctor and Donna arrive – and together they defeat the plans of the brutal Sontaran General Staal to turn the whole of Earth into a Sontaran Cloneworld.

You'd think the Doctor might have met his own daughter before, but things are never simple where the Doctor's concerned. Donna and Martha are as amazed as the Doctor to see Jenny created from cells from the Doctor's hand: she's his daughter. Jenny saves the Doctor from being shot, and seems to die herself instead as she takes the bullet. One day the Doctor is sure to discover she's not actually dead.

Just as one day he's sure to discover the truth about his friendship with the mysterious River Song. She's met the Doctor before – lots of times. Trouble is, he's not yet met her.

The Doctor has had so many friends and companions in his travels, and soon he's going to need their help again. Captain Jack, Martha, Donna, Sarah Jane Smith... They are all friends who would drop anything to return and help the Doctor.

## Rose's Warning

But one person the Doctor knows he can never see again is Rose Tyler. Not ever. It's just totally impossible as she's trapped in another universe and there can never be a route between the two.

So when Rose gives Donna a message for the Doctor, he can be sure that things are getting serious, serious and dangerous.

Especially as the message is just two words – but two words he and Rose have encountered before:

# Bad Wolf.

## Top Five Alien Encounters

### 1. The Empress of the Racnoss.
This giant arachnid ruined Donna's wedding day, but opened her eyes to the existence of life on other planets.

### 2. The Adipose.
These fat little alien babies helped Donna track down the Doctor again.

### 3. Planet of the Ood.
Donna helped the Doctor save the Ood from slavery, on her first trip to an alien planet.

### 4. The Trickster's Beetle.
A parallel world where she had never met the Doctor was created around Donna, when she visited a strange fortune teller.

### 5. Time Lord
Donna temporarily becomes part-alien herself, when a biological metacrisis makes her half Time Lord and creates a duplicate Doctor!

## DONNA

### Did you know?
The Doctor and Astrid Peth met Donna's grandad, Wilf, when they teleported down to Earth from the Titanic!

Donna Noble initially turned down the Doctor's invitation to travel with him after he rescued her from the Empress of the Racnoss. She soon regretted her decision though and began to investigate strange goings-on, in the hope of bumping into him again. Her compassion in helping the Ood and the people of Pompeii proved to the Doctor what a valuable companion she is to him.

# MARTHA

When Martha Jones agreed to go on one trip with the Doctor, as a thank you for helping him on the Moon, she didn't expect to spend a year of her life travelling through time and space with him. Martha was in love with the Doctor, but realised he did not feel the same way about her. After helping him and Captain Jack to defeat the Master, she decided to stay at home with her family, but not before giving him her mobile phone so she could always contact him.

## Top Five Bravest Moments

### 1. On the Moon.
When the hospital she worked in was abducted by aliens, Martha proved her companion potential when she stayed calm and helped the Doctor defeat the Plasmavore.

### 2. Protector.
Martha looked after the Doctor when he disgusied himself as a human, in order to escape the Family of Blood.

### 3. Walking the Earth.
It took Martha 365 days to walk around the world alone and spread the message that would save the Doctor from the Master.

### 4. Going home.
Martha loved travelling with the Doctor, so it was a huge decision for her to stay behind.

### 5. UNIT
Now Martha works as a doctor for UNIT, helping to defend the Earth against alien threats.

## Did you know?
Martha got engaged to another doctor, Tom Milligan, who she originally met when fighting the Master. When the Earth went back in time to before they had met, Martha remembered him and went back to find him.

## Top Five Bad Wolf Messages

### 1. Graffiti
On several of their adventures, Rose and the Doctor saw the words 'Bad Wolf' graffitied around them – even on the outside of the TARDIS.

### 2. Blaidd Drwg
Blon Fel Fotch Pasameer-Day Slitheen named her Welsh nuclear power station Bad Wolf and the Doctor realised the phrase was cropping up more and more on their travels.

### 3. Daleks
The Bad Wolf Corporation on the Game Station was a front for a Dalek plot to take over the world.

### 4. Parting
When Rose and the Doctor said goodbye at Bad Wolf Bay in Norway, they thought that was the last time they'd ever see each other...

### 5. Mysterious stranger
Donna has no idea who Rose is when she meets her in the alternative time line created by the Trickster Beetle but agrees to pass on her message to the Doctor. Two words: Bad Wolf.

# ROSE

### Did you know?
In the parallel world she has been living in, Rose has gained a baby brother called Tony.

Rose didn't hesitate to join the Ninth Doctor on his TARDIS travels after he rescued her from the alien Autons. They had many amazing adventures together, until Rose was tragically trapped in another universe while they were saving the Earth from a Dalek and Cybermen invasion. When Rose reappeared in our universe and gave Donna a message to pass on to the Doctor, he knew something was very, very wrong...

Donna, Martha and Rose aren't the only people to have travelled with the Doctor and when he found himself in one of the most dangerous situations he's ever faced, they were all quick to help out where they could.

# Captain Jack Harkness

The Doctor met Captain Jack back when he was working as a con man during the Second World War. The Time Lord and the former Time Agent became great friends, and Jack has been an important part of many of the Doctor's adventures.

Since Rose looked into the Time Vortex and brought Jack back to life, he cannot die and it is thought that he may one day become the ancient Face of Boe!

# Mickey Smith

Mickey was Rose's boyfriend when he and the Ninth Doctor first met. He wasn't thrilled at his girlfriend running off with an alien, but when he had the chance to travel in the TARDIS for himself, he soon saw why she chose to explore the universe.

When they visited a parallel Earth and saved London from the Cybermen, Mickey decided to stay behind and fight against them across the world.

# Sarah Jane Smith

Sarah Jane knew the Third Doctor when she was an investigative journalist in her twenties. She had always wondered what had happened to him, so was thrilled to run into him many years later when they were both looking into a mystery in a London school.

She turned down the chance to travel with him again but has had plenty of alien adventures of her own here on Earth.

# THE NEXT COMPANION?

It can be very lonely being the last of the Time Lords, so the Doctor much prefers to have companions to travel with him on his adventures. You never know when the TARDIS might land near you, so be prepared to become the Doctor's next companion with these top tips...

## 1. Be brave

When the Judoon stole a hospital and took it to the Moon, Martha Jones was calm and collected while her friend Julia cried in a corner. Guess who the Doctor took travelling?

## 2. Be curious

Donna knew the best way to find the Doctor was to investigate anything out of the ordinary and hope that if aliens were involved, the Doctor wouldn't be far behind...

## 3. Don't change time

Rose couldn't resist saving her dad's life when they went back in time to see him before he died. Her actions opened up a wound in time and he had to sacrifice himself to restore things to how they should have been and prevent the Reapers destroying Earth.

## 4. Be prepared

Although the TARDIS has a massive wardrobe, Donna packed for every eventuality when she decided to go exploring with the Doctor. She even took her passport along, just in case...

## 5. Keep up the good work

Even though they all chose not to continue travelling with the Doctor, Sarah Jane, Captain Jack and Martha still work hard to fight aliens here on Earth.

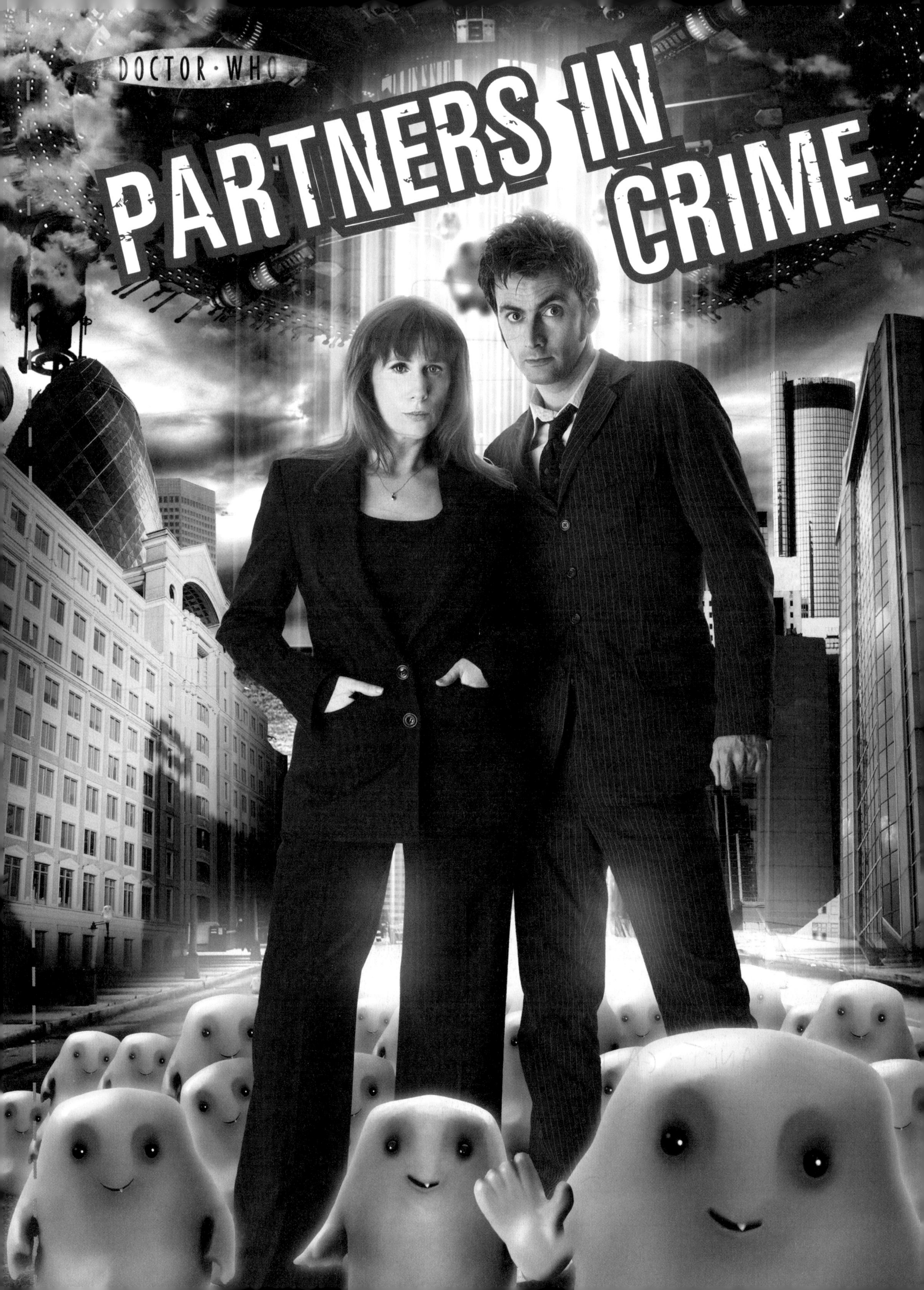
DOCTOR WHO
PARTNERS IN CRIME

# SUPER SONIC

CROSS OUT THE WORD SONIC WHEREVER IT APPEARS IN THIS GRID TO REVEAL A MESSAGE.

```
S O N I C T H S O N I C
E P L S O N I C A N E T
G A L L S O N I C I F R
S O N I C E S O N I C Y
W A S O N I C S D E S T
R S O N I C O S O N I C
Y E D S O N I C I N T H
S O N I C E T S O N I C
I M S O N I C E W A R .
```

THE MESSAGE IS:

THE - PLANET - GALLIFREY

WAS - DESTROYED - IN -

THE - TIME - WAR

# MALCASSAIRO

## INTRODUCTION

Malcassairo is a cold, dark planet situated in a far corner of the universe. In the year 100 trillion the last remaining humans took refuge there.

Travellers should note: this planet is not suitable for inexperienced tourists. Local inhabitants are aggressive and by the time you get there, there may be no other humans on the planet.

We recommend checking with your nearest interplanetary tourist information board before visiting. However, if you suddenly find yourself on the planet's wastelands, you will probably have arrived there by accident – so read on to increase your chances of survival.

### ESSENTIAL INFORMATION

Savage humanoids with sharp teeth called the Futurekind share the planet with human refugees. Ruled by a Chieftain, these creatures hunt humans for food.

### WHAT TO DO IF YOU MEET THE FUTUREKIND

Run! These fierce, sharp-fanged barbarians attack anyone they come into contact with. If they see you, they will give chase. So it is best to get away from them – and fast!

## ON ARRIVAL

As quickly as you can, make your way to the rocket silo – it is a safe base that is guarded day and night. By showing them your teeth, the guards will realise you are not one of the Futurekind. So be prepared to smile nicely.

Make contact with a man called Professor Yana – he is launching a rocket that will help the last remaining humans (and you!) to escape the planet and reach a place called Utopia.

## DID YOU KNOW?

A race of blue insectoids called the Malmooth once inhabited Malcassairo. At the time of writing, only one of the Malmooth still survives – a female called Chantho.

## DON'T MISS

The silo, the Malmooth Conglomeration

## AVOID

The Futurekind, the wastelands

# To the Doctor — a Daughter

When *Doctor Who* started — way back in 1963 — the very first episode was called *An Unearthly Child*. That unearthly child was the Doctor's grand daughter, Susan, who travelled with him in the TARDIS. Since then the Doctor has mentioned his family only a few times, but we have never met any more of his relatives. Until now.

The Doctor has a daughter — and it's as much of a shock to him as it is to everyone else!

The Doctor, Donna and Martha arrive in the middle of a war. It seems like it's been going on for years — humans battling against a race called the Hath in the tunnels below the surface of an alien planet. But in fact the war only started last week. Each side is using special progenation machines to produce new soldiers from a sample of skin taken from the back of the hand. The cells are split, then recombined to form a new person based on the original. So generations of soldiers have been born, fought, and died in just a few days...

Since they have been fighting for generations, they've forgotten why the war started. In fact it grew from an argument over a game of cards. 'The Breath of Life' is now the prize in the war — it's the thing that the humans and the Hath are fighting for. They think it is a great mythical prize — the sigh of an ancient supreme being captured after she created the Universe itself... What neither of them know is that it is actually a device for changing the planet so it can be colonised. The progenation machines were supposed to create the first colonists...

Both sides need as many soldiers as they can get. So as soon as the TARDIS arrives, the Doctor is forced to put his hand into one of the progenation machines, and has a skin sample taken. From that, the machine creates a beautiful woman. The Doctor calls the woman created from his tissue sample a 'genetic anomaly'. Donna adapts that to give her the name Jenny.

Since the Doctor's cells and genes were the template she was made from, Jenny is technically his daughter. The Doctor takes a while to come to terms with this, but he and Jenny have a lot more in common than just their genes and having two hearts each. They are both extraordinary — clever and intelligent, brave and caring. And neither of them has a home or a name.

Unlike the Doctor, Jenny was created to be a soldier. So she is incredibly strong and athletic. She's able to dodge laser beam defences by jumping, diving, cartwheeling and flipping through them.

At first, the Doctor doesn't really get on with Jenny. He's not too happy that she calls him an 'aimless, nameless space gypsy' either. It takes Donna to point out to him that he has a responsibility to her, and to bring them closer together. When Jenny helps them escape and risks her life to help find the mysterious 'Breath of Life' the Doctor realises how similar they are.

But that realisation is a painful one. Jenny reminds the Doctor of what he used to have — what he has lost. Jenny wants to travel with the Doctor, but he's not sure he can face the pain and the anger of remembering his family every time he looks at her.

Finally, though, the Doctor accepts Jenny for what she is. He comes to respect her abilities and her character and grows to like her. Certainly, for all her questions and doubts, Jenny likes and respects the Doctor — and is willing to die for him. She throws herself in front of a shot meant for the Doctor, taking the bullet for him.

As Jenny lies dying in the Doctor's arms, he tells her how amazing she is. He promises her that if she lives he'll take her with him and show her the incredible sights of the Universe. He hopes against hope that — like him — she will be able to regenerate and survive. He hopes in vain...

Then, after the Doctor, Donna and Martha have gone, something happens. Maybe it's Jenny's inherited Time Lord biology, but more likely it's something to do with 'The Breath of Life'— the gases and chemicals released to bring new life to the planet. Jenny wakes from death.

She takes a space shuttle and heads out into the Universe. In search of adventure — in search of endangered planets to save, great civilisations to rescue, monstrous creatures to defeat.

# Just like her father.

# THE OOD-SPHERE

## INTRODUCTION

If you are ever in the Horsehead Nebula, make sure you visit the Ood-Sphere.

This snow-covered planet has breathtaking views and dramatic ice plains – but it is very cold, so wrap up warm. Make sure you pack gloves, a scarf and sensible protection for winter weather.

The Ood-Sphere is the home planet of the Ood – the creatures that make life in the 42nd century a whole lot easier for humans.

Want to buy an Ood? Ood Operations, the company that ships Ood out to three different galaxies, is based here too.

## ESSENTIAL INFORMATION

If you see an Ood with bright red eyes, report the sighting immediately to an official at Ood Operations. 'Red-Eye' means that the Ood has been infected – and it could be dangerous!

## WHAT TO DO THERE

Ood Operations will gladly show you around – but certain areas are closed to the public for health and safety reasons. Ood Operations are keen to point out that, at present, due to on-going maintenance, the warehouses are not suitable for visitor tours and are strictly out of bounds.

### DID YOU KNOW?

Nearby planet the Sense-Sphere is also worth a visit if you have time.

### DON'T MISS

The views, The Song of the Ood – it's beautiful

### AVOID

Red-Eye Ood, Ood Operations warehouses

# MONSTER MASH

THE TOPS AND BOTTOMS OF THESE MONSTERS HAVE GOT ALL MUDDLED. CAN YOU MATCH EACH PIECE TO THE CORRECT OTHER HALF?

A

B

C

1

2

3

D

E

4

5

# Know Your Enemy
# MAX CAPRICORN

Max Capricorn was (quite literally) the head of Max Capricorn Cruiseliners. When things went wrong with the business, he planned to crash one of his ships, the Titanic, into Earth. Max would have survived, safe inside his Omnistate Impact Chamber, but Earth and the ship would have been destroyed.

Protective glass case

Wires connected his severed head to the life-support system

Mobile life-support system

Much older than he looked — Max had been running the company for 176 years!

Industrial wheels

Leathery skin

Fed through a Probic Vent in the back of their necks — it's their only weak spot

Full protective military uniform

Swagger stick has many uses, including activating their teleports and disabling their foes

## Know Your Enemy
# SONTARANS

The Sontarans are a clone race, dedicated to warfare and to defeating their enemies, the Rutans. They planned to use the ATMOS satellite navigation system as a weapon to change Earth's atmosphere, making it suitable for them to clone billions of troops for their battles.

# THE HATH

Humans and Hath were fighting for control of the planet Messaline but neither realised that the many generations that had died before them had only existed over the previous week. The Doctor brought peace to the planet by helping them find the 'Source' - a terraforming device that transformed the barren land into one habitable by both races.

Bubbling speech with water-filled tube instead of a mouth

Half fish, half human

Created from DNA from the previous generation

Hath soldiers wear full military uniform.

29

Made entirely of living fat converted from humans

Just a baby of its species

Born with sharp fang

Weighs about a kilo

# Know Your Enemy
# ADIPOSE

In a crisis it can also convert bone, hair and internal organs

When the Adiposian First Family lost their breeding planet, they turned to Earth to produce their next generation of offspring. They had planned to seed millions of Adipose, but only 10,000 were born before the Doctor put a stop to their plans.

# Know Your Enemy
# PYROVILE

The Pyrovile slept beneath the city of Pompeii for thousands of years, until an earthquake woke them. They formed a psychic bond with the soothsayers of the city and planned to create a Pyrovile civilisation on Earth.

Eyes and mouth
burn with fire

Can turn people to ash
with its fiery breath

The High Priestess of the Sybilline Sisterhood
was turned to stone by the Pyrovile.

Body is made of stone held
together with magma

Vulnerable to water

Multifaceted eyes

About 8ft tall

Species comes from a hive
in the Silfrax galaxy

Leaves a morphic
residue behind
when changes form

# Know Your Enemy
# VESPIFORM

Venomous stinger
can be replaced
after use

For forty years Lady Eddison kept the son she had to an alien Vespiform a secret,
only admitting the truth when her son discovered what he really was and began to
murder the guests at his mother's country mansion.

Black and silver
Dalek base

Sees through an
artificial eye

Metallic hand always
poised over control panel

New Dalek race created
from cells of his body

## Know Your Enemy
# DAVROS

The Doctor believed that Davros, the Kaled scientist and original creator of the
Daleks, had died in the first year of the Time War. He saw his command ship fly
into the jaws of the Nightmare Child at the gates of Elysium and tried to rescue
him. The Doctor failed, but Dalek Caan went back and was able to save him...

# THE Sarah Jane ADVENTURES

Sarah Jane Smith knows a lot about life beyond the stars. She spent her younger years travelling through space and time with her old friend, the Doctor, helping him defeat alien threats and defend Earth from extraterrestrial attack. Having parted company with him many years ago, she returned to her old job as a journalist. However, a recent run-in with the Time Lord gave her new confidence, and she's now back fighting aliens once more – with a little help from Maria, Luke and Clyde.

Scanner watch detects alien life and identifies species

Sonic lipstick can open locked doors and activate alien devices

Wears sensible yet stylish outfits

34

# SARAH JANE'S FRIENDS

MARIA JACKSON

After her parents split up, Maria moved to Bannerman Road with her dad, Alan. However, she had no idea of the kind of adventures that would be awaiting her. Following a chance encounter with Sarah Jane Smith, the mysterious journalist who lives across the road from her, Maria found herself battling monsters, foiling alien plots and helping to save the planet.

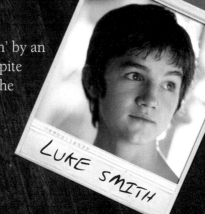

LUKE SMITH

Luke looks like any other teenage boy, but he's very special. He was 'grown' by an evil alien race called The Bane as part of their plan to take over Earth. Despite having a vast intelligence, and a mind capable of storing millions of facts, he is still learning how to behave like a normal human teenager. Sarah Jane adopted Luke as her own son, and he now lives with her.

CLYDE LANGER

Clyde started at Park Vale School at the same time as Maria and Luke. Like Maria, his parents are separated and he only recently moved to the area. Even though Clyde is different to them in many ways, they get along famously. He is streetwise, laid-back and confident, and is now a vital member of Sarah Jane's gang – even if he occasionally takes liberties.

Mr Smith is a highly advanced computer system who provides Sarah Jane with facts and figures about alien species from across the universe. He is cunningly concealed in her attic, but at first no one was sure where he came from. During one of her adventures, Sarah Jane found out that he is, in fact, a Xylok – one of a crystalline race that crashed to Earth thousands of years ago.

MR SMITH

A super-intelligent robot dog, K-9 travelled with the Doctor for many years, helping him defeat dozens of alien enemies. When Sarah Jane ran into her old Time Lord friend recently and they battled the Krillitane, he gave her a new model of her own. Sadly, she has been unable to see much of her faithful companion as he's busy sealing off a black hole.

K-9

# SARAH JANE

**THE BANE**

## DID YOU KNOW?

Bane Mothers have been known to eat their young if they fail them.

With the help of a highly addictive drink called Bubble Shock!, Mrs Wormwood, her son Davey, and the enormous and terrifying Bane Mother – who lived on the factory ceiling – planned to take over Earth. The scheming aliens, who had disguised themselves as humans, built Luke, a child 'Archetype', as a way for them to improve their drink's formula. Using Bubble Shock! they controlled people's minds. That is, until Sarah Jane drove a bus through the side of their factory and sent them packing!

The most infamous family on Raxacoricofallapatorius, the Slitheen, returned to Earth with a wicked plan to steal all of the planet's energy – and even drain the Sun of its power. When mysterious new buildings started springing up all over the place – including one at Park Vale School – Sarah Jane quickly rumbled the family, who had disguised themselves as teachers. But it wasn't until she discovered their one weakness that she was able to defeat them. With the aid of several bottles of vinegar, Miss Smith and the kids got to work on the extraterrestrial thugs.

**THE SLITHEEN**

## DID YOU KNOW?

The Slitheen collars create a compression field so they can squeeze themselves inside human skins.

**THE GORGON**

## DID YOU KNOW?

Both Sarah Jane and Bea have met a Sontaran – and they agree they look like potatoes!

Stories of visitations from spooky nuns at a local nursing home aroused Sarah Jane's interest, and she paid a visit to Lavender Lawns where she met Bea, one of its oldest residents. Bea possessed an ancient talisman that was actually a portal to another world. A nearby order of nuns who faithfully served their abbess – really a Gorgon – were trying to lay their hands on the talisman so they could get the creature back to its home planet. When Maria's dad was temporarily turned to stone, Sarah Jane and the gang raced into action to stop them doing any more damage.

# S ENEMIES

When a new laser-tag centre, Combat 3000, opened near Sarah Jane, and she discovered twenty-four kids had gone missing, her suspicions were aroused. Combat 3000's manager, Mr Grantham, and his alien boss, General Kudlak, were out to recruit new soldiers for an alien war. However, when Sarah Jane managed to get aboard Kudlak's ship and met his war-hungry leader, The Mistress, she discovered a shocking truth about the war these aliens had been fighting for hundreds of years.

THE UVODNI

## DID YOU KNOW?

The Uvodni were part of a planetery alliance battling the Malakh.

THE TRICKSTER

## DID YOU KNOW?

The Graske, agents of the Trickster, come from the planet Griffoth and can transmat through time and space.

The Trickster is one of the most slippery aliens Sarah Jane has ever encountered. He exists outside space and time and loves nothing more than to cause mayhem in the Universe. With the help of a Graske, he travelled back to 1964 and swapped a teenage Sarah Jane with her friend, Andrea, who had drowned when she fell off a pier. Suddenly, Sarah Jane no longer existed. To prevent a meteor crashing into Earth and restore order to the world, Maria went back to the Sixties, took on the faceless Trickster, and made sure that Sarah Jane was safely returned.

It looked like Luke wasn't created by aliens, but was the kidnapped son of a distraught couple who were appealing for his return. However, once they'd got hold of the lad they revealed they were actually Slitheen in disguise. But it ran deeper than that... Mr Smith, keen to awaken his fellow Xylok buried deep within Earth's core, had drafted in the Slitheen to keep Luke away from Sarah Jane, so that he could harness the lad's telekinetic powers. With Sarah Jane's computer turned against her, it fell to her old pal K-9 to save the day, and with the kids lending a hand, order was restored.

THE XYLOK

## DID YOU KNOW?

A tiny piece of Xylok crystal was freed when the volcano Krakatoa erupted, forming the mind of Mr Smith.

# TRAPPED!

Sarah Jane, Maria, Luke and Clyde are trapped in a Combat 3000 maze. Help them find their way out, before Kudlak recruits them to his army.

# THE Sarah Jane ADVENTURES

# TIME LORD TRUE OR FALSE?

SOME OF THE FACTS BELOW ARE TRUE AND SOME ARE FALSE. USE WHAT YOU'VE LEARNT ABOUT THE TIME LORDS TO DECIDE WHICH IS WHICH.

1. Time Lords have two hearts. *True*

2. They also have a hidden third eye. *False*

3. Time Lords come from the planet Gallifrey. *True*

4. Gallifrey was destroyed in the Time War. *True*

5. There was only one sun in the Gallifreyan sky. *False*

6. The current Doctor is the eleventh. *False*

7. TARDIS stands for *True* Time and Relative Direction in Space.

8. The Genesis Ark was a Time Lord prison. *True*

POLICE PUBLIC CALL BOX

POLICE TELEPHONE
FREE
FOR USE OF
PUBLIC
ADVICE & ASSISTANCE
OBTAINABLE IMMEDIATELY
OFFICER & CARS
RESPOND TO ALL CALLS
PULL TO OPEN

# Intergalactic Guide to Planets and Places:

# POMPEII

## INTRODUCTION

Heading for ancient Rome? Why not take a look at the city of Pompeii while you're there? It's only a few hours away, although you should be careful to check what year you're visiting.

Pompeii sits at the bottom of Mount Vesuvius. According to Earth history, the mountain erupts on 24th August 79AD.

It's best to visit any time before that or the city will be hidden under ash and rubble. Because of this, the city was lost for nearly 1700 years. Try to avoid the day Vesuvius erupted, because it was a dangerous place to be.

### ESSENTIAL INFORMATION

Horrific creatures called Pyroviles live deep inside Vesuvius. They want to turn human beings into Pyroviles like themselves and make Earth their home.

## WHAT TO DO THERE

The soothsayers of Pompeii can see the future. Why not ask them what the future holds for you? Their predictions are extremely accurate – so don't ask them anything you don't want to know.

## DID YOU KNOW?

The language spoken in 1st century Pompeii is Latin. Of course, if you are visiting in the TARDIS you won't have to worry about the language – as the Time Lord ship will translate everything for you.

## DON'T MISS

Try the local food – ask for ants in honey or stuffed dormouse – delicious!

## AVOID

The dust (it will turn you into stone), Mount Vesuvius, Pyroviles

# Once Upon a Time...

The way the Doctor read a book was rather different from the way Donna did. Not that she read many books, but even so she tended to read a page, then turn over and start on the next one. The Doctor riffled through the book, allowing the pages to blur past him.

'Thought you were going to read that,' Donna said.

'Yeah.' He grinned at her. 'I just did.'

'Never!'

'Oh yes.'

'What – just then?'

'It's a collection of short stories. I like short stories.' The Doctor jumped up from the seat close to the TARDIS console and busied himself with the controls. 'Yes, that's nicely calibrated itself now.'

'Let me get this right,' Donna said. 'You just read a whole book of short stories? Just like that? In about seven seconds flat?'

The Doctor nodded. 'Well, long stories take a bit longer. But, yes. There was one about a unicorn who didn't believe in people. Bit odd that, because unicorns most definitely do believe in people. You ask them. "People?" they say. "Oh yes, they're the things that stand on their back legs and go on about global warming and football." And I just smile and explain about cricket and the weather.'

He picked up the book and tossed it over to Donna. 'You'd like that one. Starts on page 72. It's called *Variations* and it's by David Banderson. It's quite short, even for a short story. Won't take you long.'

'Longer than you,' Donna said. But she sat down and opened the book.

'You're right, it's good,' Donna said. 'But it's not about unicorns.'

'Well not to begin with,' the Doctor agreed. 'It's this bloke who wants to be a writer and his mind is a blank, then his computer starts talking to him.'

'That's right.'

'And these unicorns come to the door and say they've just moved into the neighbourhood – '

'Hang on, hang on.' Donna stopped him. 'I don't know what story you're on about but it isn't that one. Not *Variations* by David Banderson. He's at his computer and it's talking to him, and then *The X Factor* comes on TV and he opens some Pringles because he's trying out a new flavour, and this woman comes in and they're happily married and she's just won the lottery…'

Donna's voice tailed off as the Doctor took the book from her and flicked through it again, just as rapidly as before.

'See,' she said.

'You're absolutely right,' the Doctor said. 'It's not about unicorns at all.'

'Told you so. Didn't I tell you so?'

'It's about a boy building a model train set.'

Donna stared at him. 'You what?'

But the Doctor was flicking through the book for a third time. 'The other stories never change,' he said. 'But now it's about a woman on a sight-seeing tour of the Serengo Ruination.' He turned to the front of the book and examined it. 'And that's a bit odd really, because this book was published a century before Serengo got ruined.'

'A bit odd?' Donna echoed. 'You're telling me the story is different every time you read it, and that's a bit odd?'

'Different every time anyone reads it,' the Doctor said. 'And that's more than a bit odd. It's pretty weird. Might even be somewhat bizarre.'

'I think it's completely bonkers.'

The Doctor considered. 'That too. Tell you what though, I can't wait to meet this David Banderson and ask him how he did it. A story that changes every time? Whatever else it might be – that's clever.'

'So we're going to see this Banderson bloke?'

The Doctor was already busy at the TARDIS controls. 'Course we are. Clever might not cover things. It's brilliant. And I want to know how it works!'

There was no answer to the doorbell.

'Maybe he's nipped out,' Donna said.

The Doctor rang the doorbell again. 'He's a writer. He creates worlds of imagination and stories that can change whenever you read them. He won't have nipped out.'

'Unless he's short of coffee.'

The Doctor thought about this. 'Hmmm,' he said. He started hammering on the door with his fist. 'Come on,' he shouted. 'David Banderson – we know you're in there. Put that pen down!'

'Or milk,' Donna said.

The Doctor stopped hammering on the door. 'You might have a point,' he conceded. 'Let's have a quick look. If he's out we can warm the kettle for him so it's all ready.'

A moment's work with the sonic screwdriver got the door unlocked and the Doctor and Donna found themselves in a nicely furnished hallway. There was a pile of letters on the floor just inside the door.

'Told you – he's down the supermarket or on holiday in the Algarve,' Donna said.

'I don't think so,' the Doctor said quietly. 'Listen.'

From somewhere in the house came the sound of someone talking quietly.

'No, no,' the voice said. 'That won't do. But perhaps if unicorns moved in next door. Or a woman went on a cruise. Or they were watching telly…'

The man was sitting at a desk, staring at his computer screen. He didn't look round as the Doctor and Donna came into the room. He didn't even seem to notice when the Doctor announced loudly:

'David Banderson, I presume? You know, your story *Variations* is just utterly brilliant.'

Donna went over to the man. 'Hey – are you all right?' She tapped him on the shoulder, but still he didn't take his eyes off the screen. On the computer was the first part of the short story Donna had read – just the opening paragraphs.

'Look, he's writing it now,' she told the Doctor. She caught sight of something else on the desk. 'Oh, that is gross!' she exclaimed. It was a bowl of what must have been fruit – apples and oranges and a few grapes. But they were grey with mould. Flies buzzed round the bowl, and Donna reached out to push it as far away as she could.

'How long has he been sitting here?' the Doctor asked quietly. 'Staring at the screen.' He waved his hand in front of the man's face.

'Or perhaps there's an earthquake,' the man said quietly, not seeming to notice. 'Or a giant bird lands outside his window and distracts him.'

'He needs something to distract him,' Donna said. 'He doesn't even know we're here.'

'The Greek gods turn out to be real, and they come round for tea,' the man said. 'No, no,' he decided. 'Been done before.'

Donna was quickly reading back through the paragraphs on the screen. As she reached the end, she realised that it must be so hard to write a story like this. There were just so many things that could happen next, so many ways the story could go. But which one to choose? Her mind was clicking through the options.

'What if his wife wins the lottery?' Donna said.

'Or he falls off his chair,' Banderson suggested.

'I know – a policeman comes to the door.'

'And it's his long lost brother.'

'Then a volcano erupts in the back garden.'

'Perhaps the trees all turn blue.'

'Or an asteroid hits Earth.'

Donna's imagination was working too fast for her to say all the things she could think of, all the stories she was seeing in her mind.

Then suddenly the Doctor was pulling her back, away from the desk. 'Donna, stop it,' he said urgently. He clicked his fingers in front of her face.

'What are you doing?'

'Stop thinking about the story,' the Doctor ordered.

'I was just trying to help,' she protested. 'Thinking of ideas. He's stuck – he's got writer's block. He's been there for days trying to work out what happens next.'

'No, no, no,' the Doctor told her. 'He hasn't got writer's block. Just the opposite. He's got too many ideas to choose from.'

'But – that's good, isn't it?'

'Good? Yes, usually. Terrific. Imagination – wonderful. Couldn't be without it. Makes the world go round. But that isn't what's happening here. Nothing's going round, except the ideas. And you were getting caught up in it too.'

'Caught?' Donna said. 'You mean – it's, like, a trap?' She looked back at David Banderson, sitting immobile in front of his computer screen, still muttering ideas and telling stories.'

The Doctor scanned Banderson with his sonic screwdriver. 'He's too far gone. We'll never snap him out of it just by distracting him.'

'But, what's happened? Why can't he just finish the story?'

The Doctor looked at Donna. He was frowning, but the frown faded into a smile, which became a grin. 'You know, you're right. You're absolutely right. He can't finish the story, because he's already under the creature's influence.'

'Hang on – creature?!'

'He can't finish it,' the Doctor said, pulling Banderson's chair away from the desk and reaching for the computer keyboard. 'But I can.'

The Doctor's fingers were a blur of speed as he typed. Text appeared on the screen and scrolled out of sight quicker than Donna could read.

'What are you doing? You're finishing it? What happens?'

'Everything!' the Doctor announced. 'Everything I can think of. Doesn't matter really, because no one will ever read it. You see in there somewhere, somehow, is a creature. You can't see it, but it's lurking inside the computer, it's in the words on the screen. A parasite that lives off the imagination. It needs stories to keep it alive.'

The words continued to blur past.

'And it's getting those stories from David Banderson while he writes this?'

'Maybe it came in from the internet. Or maybe it was always there. Probably we'll never know. But Banderson's terrific imagination woke it up and fed it. Now it wants more and more and more. It'll keep him just sitting there, inventing ideas and plots and stories until he starves or drops dead of exhaustion. You too, if I hadn't been here to stop it.'

'Oh, charming.' Donna looked at Banderson. He seemed pale and emaciated. But he had stopped muttering and was looking around in a dazed manner.

'I need to bring it to the surface,' the Doctor said as he typed. 'Draw it right into the words, inside them, living there and feasting on the fruits of my prodigious imagination so none of it is left lurking in the software or the network. Is that how you spell "prodigious"?' he wondered. 'Never mind. Doesn't matter.'

'So what do you do when you've got it all into the words?'

'This!' With a flourish, the Doctor hit a combination of keys and the printer on the desk whirred into life. As the first pages of the story printed out, the Doctor selected all the text in the file.

'And then – this!' He hit the 'delete' key.

The window went blank.

The Doctor closed the window, and then deleted the file called *Variations*. 'Gotcha,' he said with satisfaction.

The milk in the fridge had gone nasty. So David Banderson made black coffee and the Doctor explained what he had done while Banderson and Donna attacked a plate of slightly soft biscuits.

'The parasite creature is trapped in the words on the printed pages.' He flicked through them, grinning. 'It's inert, but still active. It can't reach out like it did before and grab ideas to feed on. It can't keep you entranced for days and weeks thinking through possible stories.'

'So it's safe, then?' Donna asked.

'Oh yes. But it still has some influence. It's still strong enough to stimulate the imagination of the reader.'

'That's what stories do,' Banderson pointed out. 'That's what the writer wants.'

'But the writer can only choose one story to end up on the page. All the others are in the imaginations of the readers. And every time someone reads this story, they won't see the actual words on the page. They'll imagine their own version of events. Read it aloud, and people will each hear their own story.'

'So, what did you type?' Donna wondered.

The Doctor shrugged. 'Doesn't matter. Whatever came into my head. My own story, from my own imagination.'

'So, tell us,' Banderson said. 'Tell us your version. What really did happen at the end of the story I started and you finished?'

'Same as happens in all the best stories,' the Doctor said.

'And what's that?' Donna asked.

'They all lived happily ever after…'

Donna laughed. 'As if!'

'That only happens in stories,' Banderson told them with a laugh.

'Oh you never know,' Donna said. 'What do you think, Doctor? They all lived happily ever after – is it possible?'

The Doctor finished his coffee and put down the mug on top of the pile of printed pages. He had a sad, faraway look in his eyes. 'It used to be,' he said quietly. 'Once upon a time…'

# Alien A-Z

## A — Adipose

Little lumps of living fat. When their breeding planet was lost, the Adiposian First Family defied the laws of the Shadow Proclamation and sent an intergalactic supernanny, Matron Cofelia, to grow a new generation on Earth, using humans as surrogates.

## B — Bannakaffalatta

A spiky-faced, red cyborg from Sto who travelled on the ill-fated Titanic spaceship. Short on stature but not on heroism, Bannakaffalatta gave his life to save his friends from the Host by blasting them with his electromagnetic pulse.

## C — CAL

CAL, or Charlotte Abigail Lux, is the central node of a computer at the heart of a planet called the Library. Her father built the planet and put her living mind inside to prevent her from dying.

## D — Daleks

The deadliest life forms in the universe. The Daleks are a race of armoured mutants from the planet Skaro. They wiped out the Time Lords in the Time War and they are the one enemy the Doctor truly fears.

## E — Editor-in-Chief

The Mighty Jagrafess of the Holy Hadrojassic Maxarodenfoe was the Editor-in-Chief of a broadcasting station called Satellite Five. This foul-fanged monster lived in sub-zero temperatures on Floor 500 and controlled all the news in the Fourth Earth Empire.

## F — Family of Blood

A group of body-snatching aliens who hunted the Doctor across the universe, forcing him to hide as a human. Their heightened sense of smell allows them to sniff out their victims and they can communicate telepathically.

**Graske G**

Ugly little aliens from the planet Griffoth who have the ability to jump through time and space. These nasty monsters travel the universe kidnapping creatures and replacing them with their own changelings.

**Hath H**

The half-fish, half-human Hath are locked in a battle for survival with humans on the planet Messaline. They have a water-filled tube instead of a mouth and talk with strange bubbling noises. Like their enemies, they use machines to grow new soldiers.

**Isolus I**

An alien race sustained and linked by love. The Isolus have drifted through space for thousands of years, but when one fell to Earth it took refuge in a human girl and used her to make children vanish.

**Jenny J**

The Doctor's daughter. Jenny was born fully-grown from a tissue sample stolen from the Doctor on the planet Messaline. She fought in the war between the Hath and humans and the Doctor thought she died saving him. But she didn't...

**Krillitane K**

Shape-shifting monsters that absorb the features of the races they defeat. For many generations they resembled bat-like creatures but on Earth they disguised themselves as human teachers. They were eventually destroyed by the Doctor's trusty robot dog K-9.

**Lazarus L**

Professor Lazarus was an elderly scientist who created a machine that reversed the effects of time. He used it to make himself young again but in doing so it corrupted his DNA and he became a hideous skeletal monster.

**Max Capricorn M**

A scary cyborg with more money than sense, Max Capricorn tried to sabotage his own company by crashing the Titanic spaceship into Earth. He employed the Host to remove all witnesses to his wicked crime.

## Novice Hame

A Catkind nun who secretly bred humans on New Earth for medical experimentation. This former Sister of Plenitude tried to redeem herself by becoming the Face of Boe's nurse. He protected her when the Bliss virus struck.

## Ood

Gentle, identical, tentacle-faced aliens bred by humans in the 42nd century to be their servants. Normally peaceful by nature, the Ood are susceptible to an infection called Red-Eye, which can turn them into rabid killers.

## Pyrovile

Fire-breathing magma creatures from the planet Pyrovilia. The Pyrovile fell to Earth and were reduced to dust. They seeded themselves into humans and tried to convert millions of them into new Pyroviles using the power of Mount Vesuvius.

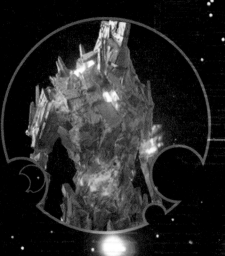

## Quarks

The Dominators' deadly robotic servants. Quarks are heavily armed with rectangular bodies and spherical crystalline heads. They forced the Dulkians to drill holes into their planet's core to get fuel for the Dominators' spaceships.

## Racnoss

Huge red creepy crawlies that originated in the Dark Times. The Racnoss are born starving and like gobbling up whole planets. The Empress of the Racnoss planned to release her hungry children on Earth so they could devour mankind.

## Sontarans

Short, stocky and brutal, the Sontarans are a military race who live for the glory of battle. Their leader General Staal tried to turn Earth into a clone world to aid them in their bloody war against the Rutans.

## The Trickster's Beetle — T

One of the Trickster's Brigade. An invisible insect which Donna encountered on the planet Shen Shan. It attaches itself to the back of its victims and changes the course of their lives.

## Usurians — U

The Usurians conquor planets through the use of economics rather than warfare. They took over the population of Earth in the far future and transported them first to Mars and then Pluto, building artificial suns around the planet to heat it. They were only stopped when the Doctor reprogrammed their computer and bankrupted them.

## Vespiform — V

Shape-shifting insectoid life forms that have hives in the Silfrax galaxy. They look like giant wasps but have the ability to disguise themselves as humans. One flew to Earth in 1885 and had a son with Lady Eddison.

## Weeping Angels — W

An ancient race of stone statues that have the power to zap their victims back in time with a single touch. They feed off chronon energy but can only move when they're not being watched.

## Xeraphin — X

The inhabitants of planet Xeriphas fled to Earth during the war between the Vardon and the Kosnax 140 million years ago. Radiation turned them into a single bioplasmic body but the Master split their personality into good and evil.

## Yeti — Y

The Yeti were a collection of servicer robots, disguised as the mythical creatures of Earth also known as the Abominable Snowmen. They were controlled by a disembodied mind calling itself the Great Intelligence.

## Zygons — Z

A refugee band of shape-shifting monsters. Their vessel crash-landed in Loch Ness after their home planet was destroyed by a stellar explosion. Zygons have suckers all over their bodies and can shoot electrical currents from their fingertips.

# Ood T-shirt

Create your own Ood uniform or T-shirt with these designs!

## You will need:

| | |
|---|---|
| A plain T-shirt | Card |
| Fabric paints or pens | Masking tape |
| Tracing paper | Scissors |
| Pencil | A grown-up with an iron |

**1.** Choose the design you want to put on your T-shirt. Place a sheet of tracing paper over it and copy the image with a pencil.

**2.** Turn the tracing paper over and shade over the traced lines with a pencil.

**3.** Put the tracing paper the right way up on top of the sheet of card and carefully draw over the traced lines again, to copy the image on to it.

**4.** Cut out the shape you have drawn to create a stencil.

**5.** Tape the stencil in place on the T-shirt, to hold it still.

**6.** Follow the instructions on your fabric paint or pen to colour in the image. Dab carefully at the edges of the stencil, to keep the image neat.

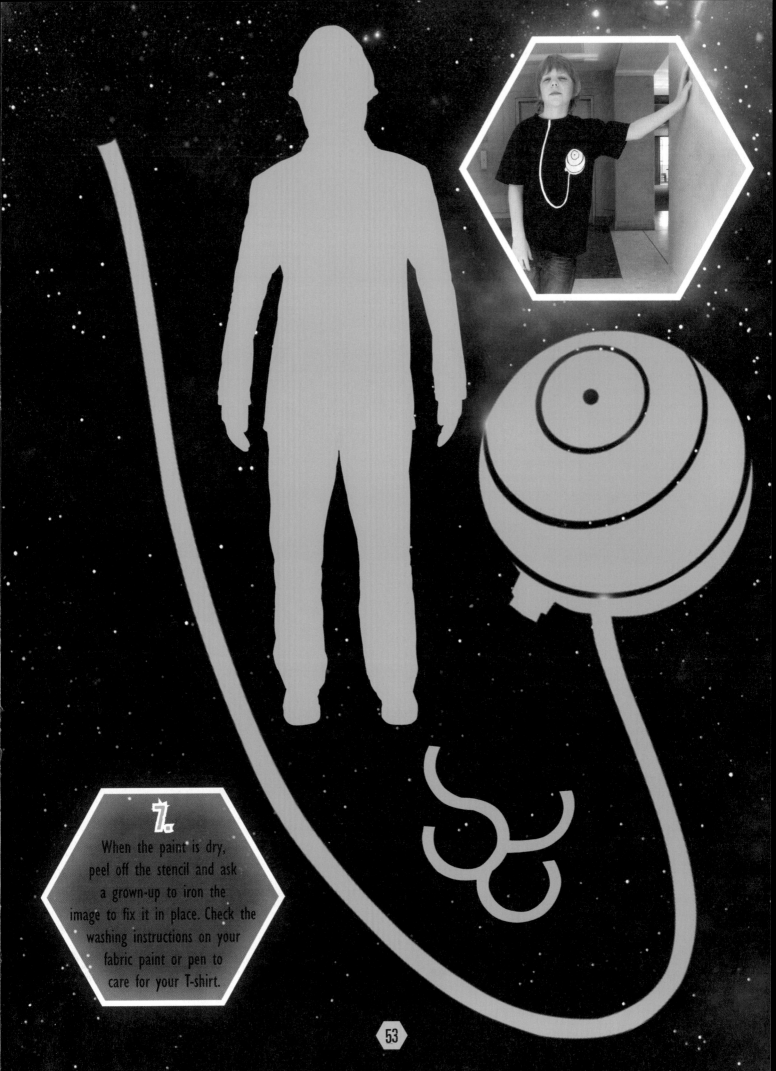

**7.**

When the paint is dry, peel off the stencil and ask a grown-up to iron the image to fix it in place. Check the washing instructions on your fabric paint or pen to care for your T-shirt.

EEERRRGHHH....

KZZKK!

The poor thing - it just **shrivelled** up...

Wasted away by the time winds. Come on, we're not **finished** yet.

LATER...

Here we are. Sentinel One and Two back up and running. They say three's a crowd, so these two will manage fine on their own.

Right then - **back on duty!**

THANK YOU, DOCTOR.

What a sad, lonely world.

It's **best** that way, Donna. The warp in Time must be **protected**. I've fixed the Force Barrier to extend **beyond** the planet itself, cutting it off the rest of Space and Time forever. Once we leave, the galaxy will be **safe** again.

Then let's go.

THE END.

# Intergalactic Guide to Planets and Places:

# MESSALINE

## INTRODUCTION

Today, the beautiful, lush planet of Messaline is very different to the planet that previously existed for thousands of years.

Originally bleak and unwelcoming with muddy bogs on the surface and dangerous tunnels underground, it wasn't the ideal place for a holiday or even a quick day trip.

When humans and creatures called Hath first wanted to colonise the planet, a war broke out between them. Each side used machines to create new soldiers, but the war only lasted a week…

## HISTORY LESSON

The humans and Hath wrongly thought that something called The Breath of Life was the sigh of an ancient supreme being after she created the Universe. But it turned out to be a device that their ancestors had brought to the planet so it could be terraformed.

## THE HATH

The Hath are strange-looking creatures that bubble and gurgle. They used to live and work with humans. Sadly that all changed when war was declared and the two different groups started fighting over an underground city, distrusting each other and creating more and more soldiers with their progenation machines.

## DID YOU KNOW?

Messaline's current beauty is due to a mixture of methane, hydrogen, ammonia, amino acids, proteins and nucleic acids. This combination was able to accelerate evolution – and was used to make this once-barren planet habitable.

## DON'T MISS

The new planet surface — it's beautiful!

## AVOID

The period before Messaline evolved, getting caught up in the war

# COSMIC CROSSWORD

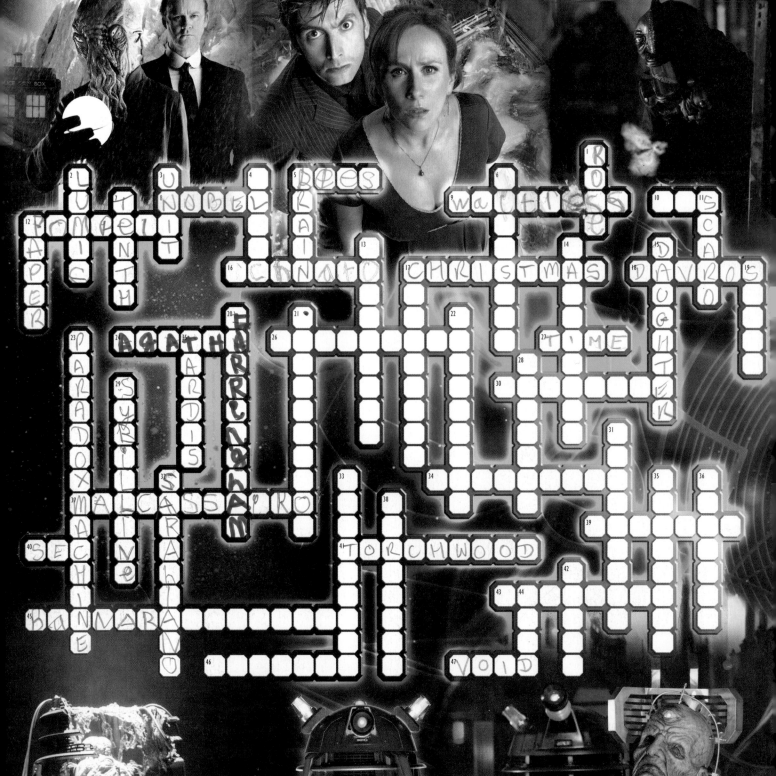

The crossword grid contains the following filled-in answers:

- NOBEL
- BEES
- WAFFLES
- R O
- POMPEII
- S
- C
- CHINA
- CHRISTMAS
- DAVROS
- AGATHA
- TIME
- PARADOX
- TARDIS
- FARRINGHAM
- MALCASSAIRKO
- SARAH
- MACHINE
- TORCHWOOD
- SECH
- BANNARA
- VOID

# ACROSS

5. These insects are going missing all over Earth (4)
8. Donna's surname (5)
9. Astrid's job (8)
10. The Doctor went on a day trip in this vehicle (3)
12. The Doctor and Donna visited this Italian city (7)
16. Professor Yana's assistant (7)
17. Max _____ tried to destroy his cruiseliner and Earth (9)
18. This scientist created the Daleks (6)
24. The Doctor and Donna met writer _____ Christie (6)
26. The planet fought over by humans and Hath (9)
27. The TARDIS can travel through _____ and space (4)
30. A creature made of rocks and magma (8)
34. The Master used this phone network to control people (9)
37. The Doctor discovered the Master living here (11)
39. An unfortunately-named cruiseliner (7)
40. This Dalek bonded with a human (3)
41. Captain Jack works for this organisation (9)
43. Family from Raxacoricofallapatorious (8)
45. This red, spiky alien was secretly a cyborg (15)
46. Creator of the Genetic Manipulation Device (7)
47. The space between universes (4)

# DOWN

1. This old friend of the Doctor's unexpectedly returns (4)
2. The creator of the Cybermen (5)
3. Martha is working for _____ when she calls the Doctor back to Earth (4)
4. The Futurekind can be identified by their pointy _____ (5)
5. The Ood are born holding this in their hands (5)
6. A planet with no life and diamond waterfalls (8)
7. The Doctor is in his _____ incarnation (5)
11. The home planet of the Daleks (5)
12. The Doctor has psychic _____ (5)
13. Round aliens with dangerous spikes (9)
14. The Master fled the Time War when the Daleks took control of this (9)
15. The Doctor was surprised when he suddenly had a _____ (8)
17. The Titanic visited Earth at this time of year (9)
19. Ood _____ was Halpen's personal slave (5)
20. The Doctor taught at this school for boys (10)
21. The SS _____ almost crashed into a sun (10)
22. A giant wasp-like alien (9)
23. The Master turned the TARDIS into this (7,7)
25. The Doctor's spaceship (6)
28. These bony aliens attempted a Christmas invasion of Earth (7)
29. The _____ Sisterhood (9)
31. The Doctor and the Master come from here (9)
32. This old companion of the Doctor's has been having adventures of her own (5,4)
33. This clone race fight against the Rutans (9)
35. The _____ Host were not as angelic as they looked (8)
36. Alien created from fat (7)
38. The Master kept the 900 year old Doctor in one of these (8)
42. The Plasmavore drank her victim's blood through one of these (5)
44. The Doctor is a Time ____ (4)

46 47 48 49 50 FINIS

45 44 43 42 41 40

22 23 24 25 26 27

21 20 19 18 17

START 1 2 3

TIME TRIP

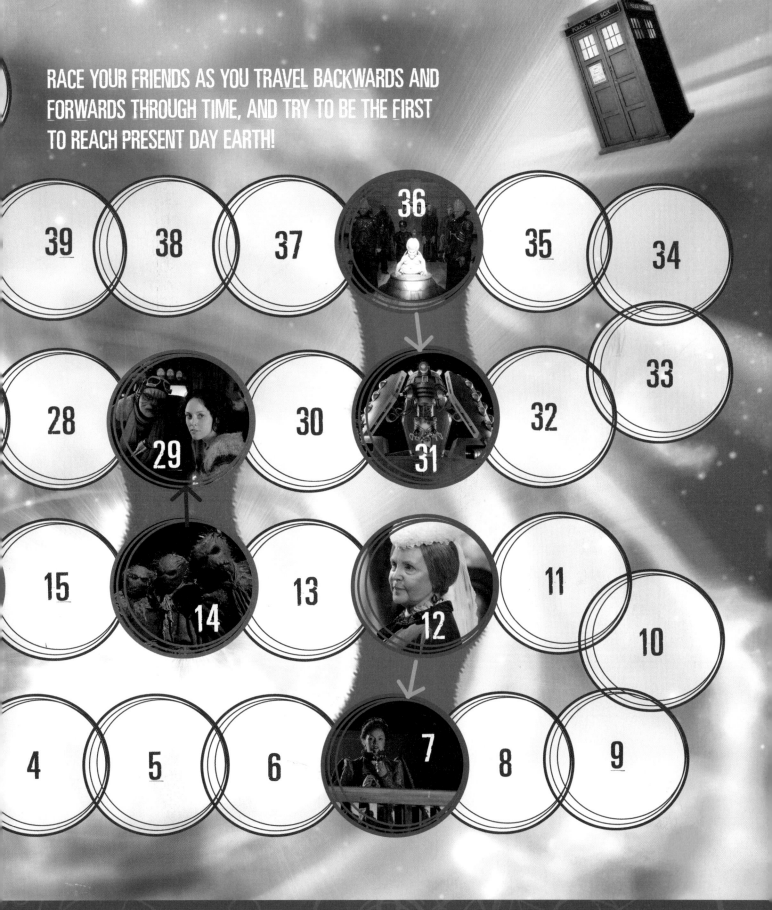

RACE YOUR FRIENDS AS YOU TRAVEL BACKWARDS AND FORWARDS THROUGH TIME, AND TRY TO BE THE FIRST TO REACH PRESENT DAY EARTH!

39 38 37 36 35 34

28 29 30 31 32 33

15 14 13 12 11 10

4 5 6 7 8 9

Roll a die to see who starts. The person to roll the highest number goes first. Players take it in turns to roll the die and move their playing pieces forward by the number of places shown on the die. If you land on a red vortex, travel forwards in time to the place shown. If you land on a blue vortex, follow it back in time to the place shown.

# BATTLE FOR SURVIVAL

**WHEN DONNA NOBLE MEETS ROSE TYLER, IT'S THE BEGINNING OF AN EPIC BATTLE. A BATTLE FOR THE SURVIVAL NOT JUST OF THE HUMAN RACE, BUT FOR THE WHOLE UNIVERSE.**

The Doctor knows things are getting serious. When Rose went into the parallel universe after helping him defeat the Daleks and Cybermen, the openings between the universes were closed forever. Or so he thought.

If cracks are appearing again in the very fabric of the Universe, then something terrible is happening… Then, just as it seems things are at their worst, Earth disappears.

For a while now, the Doctor and Donna have been hearing about planets that are 'lost'. Pyrovillia, the Adipose breeding planet, and now Earth itself. Not destroyed, but literally lost – moved across space to a distant corner of the Universe. What force could be powerful enough to shift whole planets? The answer is a terrifying one:

## RETURN OF THE DALEKS

At the heart of a web of the lost planets, the Dalek command ship – The Crucible – controls a whole new Dalek Fleet. But these are different from the other Daleks the Doctor and his friends have encountered since the creatures were all but destroyed in the Great Time War.

The Dalek race was saved from oblivion by a lone, mad source. The last survivor of the Cult of Skaro – Dalek Caan.

## DALEK CAAN'S STORY

Dalek Caan used an emergency temporal shift to escape from the Doctor after he defeated them in 1930s New York. Using the very last of his reserves of power, Caan went back in time to save the one person who could help rebuild the Dalek race.

Caan flew unprotected into the heart of the Great Time War. Like Rose, when she absorbed the Time Vortex, Dalek Caan saw the whole of time. Its infinite complexity and majesty raged through his mind. And it drove him mad…

But Caan achieved his mission. He went back to the very first year of the Great Time War. To the moment when Davros, creator of the Daleks, was killed as his command ship flew into the jaws of the Nightmare Child at the Gates of Elysium. He saved Davros.

## DAVROS

Thousands of years ago, on the planet Skaro, Davros created the Daleks. He was a brilliant scientist looking for a way for his people – the Kaleds – to survive. The Kaleds had been at war with the Thals for a thousand years, and were mutating because of the chemical, biological and nuclear weapons used early in that war.

Davros worked out what the Kaleds would eventually become, and designed an armoured travelling life-support system for that creature. The Dalek. But he also changed the genetic make-up – eliminating the 'weaker' emotions and making them desperate to survive at any cost. Even if it meant conquering every other race in the Universe to ensure they would survive to the end of time.

Davros was a brilliant genius. But he was also completely mad.

When Dalek Caan rescued Davros from the Great Time War, the scientist immediately set about creating a new race of Daleks. He took cells from his own body and grew them into Dalek creatures. The Daleks were reborn – to conquer and exterminate!

## THE REALITY BOMB

But just as they had done before, once the Daleks no longer needed Davros, they discarded him. They confined him to the lower levels of The Crucible – the Vaults – where they kept him and the deranged remains of Dalek Caan. The Daleks were led by one of their own – a new Supreme Dalek that directed their every move, and even organised the capture of the greatest enemy of the Daleks: the Doctor. And when the new Supreme Dalek had finished with the Doctor and his friends, they were sent to join Davros. As his playthings.

The Daleks were concentrating on their great plan to destroy all other life in the Universe. They ignored the prophecies of Dalek Caan – the one Dalek who had seen into the depths of time itself. They didn't believe that even the Doctor could stop them from using their most powerful and deadly weapon ever. The Reality Bomb.

This was a weapon powered by the exact configuration of the planets they had stolen, and which they now linked together in a huge web generating tremendous energy. Enough energy to counter out the electrical fields that hold everything together. Everything in the Universe. The Daleks can unravel reality itself.

## THE CHILDREN OF TIME

The Doctor has always benefited from the help and ingenuity of his friends and they are united in their desire to protect Earth and save the Universe itself. They're brought together by another old friend of the Doctor's – former Prime Minister, Harriet Jones. She sacrifices her life bringing them all together to fight the Daleks…

Dalek Caan calls them the Children of Time. And he knows that one of them will die…

It's not only Rose who returns to battle the Daleks. Her mum, Jackie and Mickey Smith are also back. Together they manage to get aboard The Crucible. Once there, they meet up with Sarah Jane Smith. She's one of the Doctor's oldest friends. With the help of her adopted son Luke and super computer 'Mr Smith' she's already on the Daleks' case. She's got something that could destroy their fleet – a Warp Star, a huge explosion waiting to happen, trapped inside a beautiful jewel…

The Doctor may be wary of Torchwood – after all, it was set up by Queen Victoria to watch out for him! But Captain Jack Harkness is in charge now, and he's one man you can depend on in a crisis. The Daleks have exterminated him before, but thanks to help from Rose and the power of the Time Vortex, they can't do it again. He's a man who simply cannot die.

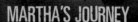

## MARTHA'S JOURNEY

Martha Jones once spent a year – a year that never was – travelling the world for the Doctor. She's got another journey to make, but not to save the world – to destroy it. Teleporting to escape the Daleks, she makes her way to an ancient castle in Germany. Deep beneath the castle is a control chamber where she can use the Osterhagen Key.

A chain of 25 nuclear warheads has been placed round the Earth, buried at strategic points in the planet's crust. If Martha and her colleagues activate their keys – the whole world will explode.

It will destroy everything, and kill everyone. But it will stop the Daleks from using their Reality Bomb…

## ANOTHER DOCTOR

Despite his hatred of war and destruction, the Doctor has a weapon too. Something that will focus the power of the Daleks' weapon back on them. But the Doctor with the weapon is not the real Doctor – it's another Doctor!

When the Doctor is finally reunited with Rose, it should be a happy moment. But instead he is blasted down by a Dalek. Helped into the TARDIS by Rose and Jack, he should regenerate. But he expels all the energy that would change his form into the hand he lost in his fight with the Sycorax Leader…

And later, when the Daleks try to destroy the TARDIS, another, duplicate Doctor is created out of that energy and the hand.

But ultimately even these terrible weapons – the sorts of weapons the Doctor always hopes never to have to use – are not enough. The Daleks are in total control… Nothing can stop them now.

Nothing, except Donna Noble.

## TIME LORD DONNA?

For a while, the Doctor has sensed that there is something extra special about Donna. Even Rose has noticed the way the Time Lines seem to converge on her. She's destined to be at the very heart of something extraordinary.

Perhaps the Ood sensed it when they called her the Doctor-Donna. She is caught up in the blast of energy that creates that second Doctor, and she absorbs it – becoming part Time Lord. A blend of the best of the two races.

Donna becomes the one person in the whole of creation who is clever enough to turn the Daleks' own weapons against themselves, and destroy them.

But that brilliance comes at a price. It's just too much for her human brain to cope with. So, to the Doctor's intense sadness, he has to wipe from Donna's mind every memory of who he is, and what she has become – of her ever meeting him, and of all the amazing things they did together. She can never remember, or it will kill her.

He doesn't just lose Donna. Rose too has to return to her own universe. But at least she is not alone. She has her mum Jackie, and someone else too – the other Doctor. Just as Donna was part Time Lord, so the 'new' Doctor was created part human. He has a single heart and a normal lifespan.

A life he and Rose can spend together.

While the Doctor – the real Doctor – travels onwards, to face new adventures and fight new battles. Alone and lonely. At least, for now.

# Most Beautiful Music

D onna settled herself into the seat beside the Doctor and looked round. The huge vaulted chamber was packed. There was not an empty seat anywhere. Men, women, dog people, giant crustaceans, all manner of aliens had their eyes – or whatever they used instead – pointed at the stage at the front of the massive auditorium.

'Maybe we should have dressed up a bit,' the Doctor said.

'Some of us have,' Donna told him.

'Oh,' he said, seeming to notice her dress for the first time. 'Yes.'

'What's that supposed to mean?'

'Don't worry,' the Doctor assured her. 'They're all here to listen not to look. We are so lucky to get a ticket.'

'You keep saying.'

'Good seats too.'

'So,' Donna said, 'apart from the most beautiful music in the universe – which Mum always told me was the Beatles anyway – what else should I watch out for? I mean, where are we? Will there be lasers and dancers and a bit where we have to hold up candles or anything?'

The Doctor leaned close and spoke quietly. 'This isn't just any old concert. It's renowned throughout the cosmos. The Concert of Most Beautiful Music at the Church of the High Exalted on Cantabulous Nine is the most famous cultural event this side of the Literary Olympics of Splatt Minor. Only staged once every ten years.'

Donna raised her eyebrows. 'Fancy. And I thought culture was something to do with yoghurt.'

The Doctor grinned. 'That's good,' he said. 'Like that. Yes. But no, nothing to do with yoghurt.'

'Why's it so special then? Best bands in the universe playing for charity or what?'

'Just one act. A child, apparently. Best in his class at the church school or something, I suppose. He plays an instrument called a lassimater. It's sort of part flute, part recorder, part didgeridoo.'

'And it makes beautiful music?'

'The most beautiful.'

'Right,' Donna said as the lights dimmed. 'Just checking.'

There was no announcement or introduction. Spotlights illuminated the stage, and a figure walked slowly and awkwardly into view.

'You said he was a child,' Donna whispered.

'He's called the Child of Music,' the Doctor replied. 'Guess I sort of assumed.'

'Shhh!' hissed someone behind Donna.

'Shh yourself,' she said loudly over her shoulder. 'Some of us are here for the music, you know.'

On the stage in front of them, an old man, bent with age, his wispy white hair clinging to his liver-spotted scalp, raised a long wooden pipe to his lips and began to blow.

There was utter silence when the music finally stopped. It seemed to take the audience several seconds to recover before the applause started.

'That was…' Donna shook her head. She wasn't sure how to describe it.

'Wasn't it?' the Doctor agreed. 'The most beautiful music – doesn't describe it really.'

'Just fantastic.'

'This is just the interval. The second half is supposed to be even better. And if we really like it,' the Doctor went on in a whisper, 'we can come back in ten years.'

They pushed their way along to the aisle and joined the mass of people heading out of the huge vaulted auditorium and out into the foyer. Monks and ministers of the Church of the High Exalted were standing by the doors, heads bowed and faces shadowed by the heavy hoods they wore.

'Right,' Donna said surveying the crowds of jostling people and life forms ahead of them. 'This bit I do understand. Lend us some dosh and I'll get the ice creams.'

There was a gift shop off the foyer, and the Doctor amused himself looking at the small plastic lassimaters and stretchy rubber figures of the 'child' playing the instrument. There were postcards showing the outside of the Church of the High Exalted drifting on its small island in the middle of the Petronic Ocean, engraved glasses and the usual guide book.

But what really caught his attention was a big coffee table book that showed photographs from all the concerts of the few last hundred years. The page corners were bent and the cover was slightly torn. It was reduced to half price.

'Interesting?' Donna asked, handing the Doctor a tub of something cold and bright green. 'I don't know what mindorolan and janissary is, but it's all that was left.'

The Doctor balanced the tub of ice cream on a nearby shelf and showed Donna the pictures in the book.

'This is three hundred and twenty years ago,' he said. 'The very first concert.'

'He really is a child,' Donna said. 'Can't be more than about six years old. I guess the name just stuck.'

'Except,' the Doctor said, turning the pages, 'ten years later he's a teenager. And ten years after than he's in his twenties.'

'So they kept him on for a bit,' Donna said through a mouthful of ice cream.

'And then some.' The Doctor kept turning the pages.

Donna stopped spooning ice cream. 'He just gets older and older.'

The Doctor nodded, still leafing through the book. 'And older and older. And then older still.'

'It's the same child. All these years. Centuries. The poor man. He must be so old.'

A bell rang to warn them the interval was nearly over. The Doctor put the book back on the shelf.

'You want my ice cream?' he asked Donna. 'I'm not really hungry.'

Donna put her half-eaten pot on the shelf beside the Doctor's. 'Me neither.'

The Doctor was right. The music in the second half was even more beautiful. But whereas before Donna had found it exhilarating and uplifting, now she felt very different. She watched the frail, withered old man on the stage in front of them, illuminated by a single pale light. And she could hear the sadness and the melancholy in the music.

By the time the concert finished, Donna's cheeks were wet with tears.

The Doctor grabbed her hand, and led her not towards the exits but against the flow of people and towards the front of the auditorium.

'Where are we going?'

'To meet the star of the show.' The Doctor jumped up on to the stage with a single bound. He turned to help Donna clamber up after him.

'You didn't say anything about running and jumping,' she said. 'I'd never have worn these heels.'

Behind the stage, they found themselves in a stone-built corridor. A hooded monk stepped in front of the Doctor and held up a hand. His voice was a rasping, throaty whisper: 'This area is restricted.'

'Not to us,' the Doctor said, holding up his psychic paper. 'President of the Child of Music's fan club. And vice president. Official business.' He pushed past.

Donna could hear the throaty shouts of the monk behind them as they hurried along. Ahead, she could see the stooped figure of the Child of Music as he was escorted down the corridor by several more of the hooded figures.

'Wait!' the Doctor shouted, breaking into a run. 'Just wanted a quick word.'

One of the hooded monks turned to block their approach. He put a black-gloved hand on the Doctor's shoulder, holding him back. The Doctor bounced and pushed and struggled to see over the cloaked shoulder.

'Just wanted to say how wonderful it was,' he called. 'The music – terrific. Absolutely brilliant. Never heard anything like it.'

The wizened old man turned slowly and nodded in appreciation. 'Thank you. You are very kind.'

'That music,' Donna added. 'It's so emotional. It does things to you.'

'Can we do anything in return?' the Doctor wondered.

The old man shuffled slowly back towards them. 'For me?' he seemed surprised.

'Yeah. That's right.' The Doctor leaned over the shoulder of the monk. 'Tell me,' he said, his tone suddenly serious. 'Really and honestly. What do you want? What do you want more than anything else?'

The old man's eyes met the Doctor's then Donna's, just for a brief sad moment. Then he slowly turned away. But she heard his answer quite clearly:

'I want to die.'

Donna picked herself up from the cold ground. 'Well, really. Thrown out of a church by a monk. Reminds me of Ginny's wedding,' she grumbled as she dusted herself down. 'So, what do we do now?'

The Doctor was examining the heavy iron door that had slammed shut behind them. 'What do you think?'

From the way he said it, Donna could guess. 'We break back in again?'

'Absolutely. We have to help that poor creature.'

'The old man?'

The Doctor looked at her like she was completely mad. 'No. The other poor creature.'

But before she could ask what he meant, he had his sonic screwdriver out and was unlocking the door.

As soon as they were back inside, the Doctor held up his sonic screwdriver. It glowed blue, the light getting brighter as he turned slowly. 'Yes – this way.'

'What creature?' Donna asked again as the Doctor led the way down a stone corridor into the heart of the ancient building.

'Inside the instrument – the lassimater.'

'There's a creature inside the musical instrument?' Donna said, surprised.

'I know. I just said that.'

The Doctor bundled Donna into an alcove, putting his hand over her mouth in warning. Moments later two of the hooded monks walked slowly past. When they were gone, the Doctor and Donna stepped out of the alcove.

'That was close,' the Doctor murmured.

'Not as close as this,' Donna said, pointing to the hooded figure that was rapidly approaching.

A gloved hand pointed, and a rasping voice shouted a warning.

'Run?' Donna suggested.

'Run,' the Doctor agreed.

They ran.

And as they ran, hooded figures close behind, the Doctor gasped out a breathless explanation: 'Don't recognise the species, but the poor creature is trapped inside the musical instrument. Been shut up inside for centuries. Since the concerts started.'

'But why?'

They turned a corner, the sonic screwdriver glowing ever brighter as they neared their destination. 'Who knows? Maybe an accident. Maybe deliberate. But now the instrument is the creature's prison.'

'And the music? The sad, beautiful music?'

They were almost at the end of the corridor – a door. A gloved hand snatched at Donna's hair as she ran. The Doctor grabbed the door, wrenched it open. He slammed it shut behind them and pointed the sonic screwdriver at it. Donna heard the clunk of the lock.

Then a second later, the sound of fists hammering on the locked door and shouts from outside.

'The music,' the Doctor said quietly, 'is the sound of the creature crying out for help. It's so very old, you see. It sleeps most of the time. It's woken only by the gentle breath of the Child of Music.'

He was speaking quietly because the old man was curled up asleep on a small bed in the corner of the room. He clutched the musical instrument, hugging it tight.

'The creature's only friend,' the Doctor went on. 'The only person who cares about it.'

'So why's he so old?'

The Doctor sat down on the edge of the bed. The old man stirred in his sleep.

'The creature sleeps so much partly to dream of escape. But also to pass on its energy and life essence to the Child.' The Doctor looked up at Donna and she could see the sadness in his eyes. 'Imagine it – a creature that can live for centuries, maybe thousands of years. And the one person it really cares about, won't live nearly that long. It can't bear the thought of outliving its friend. A bit like…' His voice tailed off.

'A bit like,' Donna finished for him, 'Puff the Magic Dragon.'

The Doctor nodded. 'Exactly what I was thinking,' he lied.

There was a loud hammering from the door now. The old man's eyes were open and he was watching the Doctor and Donna warily.

'We're here to help,' the Doctor assured him. He gently lifted the lassimater from the old man's gnarled hands. 'May I?'

'You can help us?' he wheezed. 'Really help us?' The old man nodded as he watched the Doctor aim the sonic screwdriver at the musical instrument. 'Yes, at last – I believe you can. After all this time.' He closed his eyes again. 'I tried to break the instrument, to let it out. But nothing I could do…' His voice was fading.

The door crashed open.

The instrument exploded, shattered fragments falling to the floor.

A bright yellow light shimmered out of the broken lassimater, dancing across the room towards a tiny window set high in the bare stone wall.

The room was filled with sound – a soaring, wonderful sound that shimmered and swelled with the glow of the light.

'It's singing,' Donna realised. 'Singing for us.'

The old man on the bed drew a final ragged breath and smiled. His last words were barely more than a sigh: 'Thank you.'

Then the light burned through the window and was gone. The last notes of the creature's song lingered in the air before they too faded away.

A hooded figure stood in front of the Doctor and Donna. More of the figures were standing in the doorway.

'What was that?' the figure asked, the rasping scrape of its voice filled with awe. 'What was that amazing noise?'

'The most beautiful music of all,' the Doctor said. 'The sound of freedom.'

# HAVE WE MET?

THE DOCTOR IS USED TO SURPRISES. EVERY DAY BRINGS A NEW ADVENTURE, NEW ALIENS, NEW PLANETS AND NEW PEOPLE TO HELP. BUT IT IS NOT OFTEN HE MEETS SOMEONE HE DOESN'T KNOW, BUT WHO KNOWS EXACTLY WHO HE IS...

## THE LIBRARY

When the psychic paper revealed the message; 'The library, come as soon as you can. x', the Doctor was quick to respond. Donna was surprised that the cry for help came with a kiss, but the Doctor thought nothing of it until a team of astronauts also showed up at the deserted library...

## RIVER SONG

The team was led by Professor River Song, an archaeologist. At first she thought the Doctor was pretending not to know her, but she soon realised that he really had no idea who she was. She was shocked – she and the Doctor went way back, but in his time, he hadn't met her yet.

## SPOILERS

River had an old diary, packed with details of her life with the Doctor. But she wouldn't let him look at it, or tell him anything about how she knew him, as she didn't want to spoil the future for him. It was his rule – he told her never to give anything away. Donna was scared though. It seemed River Song had never met her in the Doctor's future.

## SCREWDRIVER

The Doctor was scared too, when he found out he'd given River his sonic screwdriver at some point in their future together. He realised how much she must mean to him when she whispered one word in his ear, to prove herself. His name. There's only one time the Time Lord could have revealed his name...

## SACRIFICE

River realised that the future Doctor, her Doctor, gave her his screwdriver knowing that she was going to die. Although she sacrificed herself in the library, in order to save the Doctor, he was also able to 'save' her. He downloaded her into the library computer, and she survives along with Charlotte Abilgail Lux and the others who died in the library.

## BUT THE MYSTERY OF WHO RIVER SONG REALLY IS REMAINS...

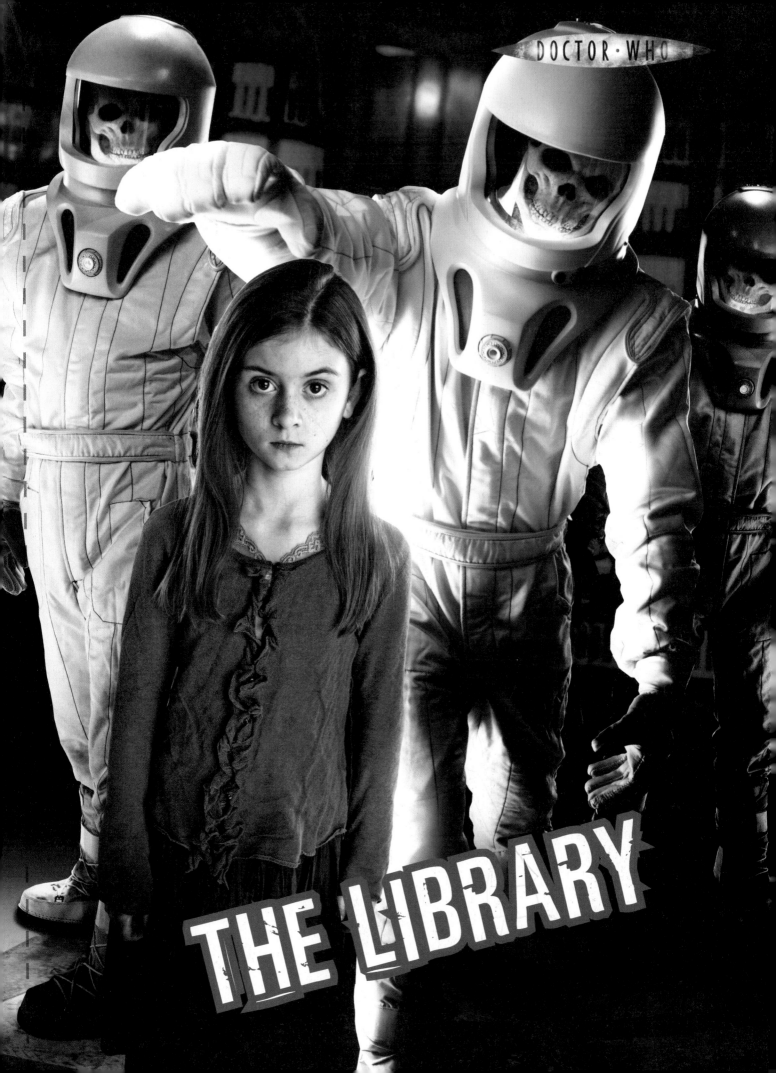

DOCTOR·WHO

THE LIBRARY

# SONIC SAVES THE DAY

THE SONIC SCREWDRIVER HAS MANY DIFFERENT USES, BUT WHAT WOULD YOU USE IT FOR? DRAW YOURSELF USING THE SONIC SCREWDRIVER TO FIX A PROBLEM OR HELP YOU ESCAPE FROM A STICKY SITUATION!

# Intergalactic Guide to Planets and Places:

# MIDNIGHT

## INTRODUCTION

Midnight is the perfect destination if you are looking for somewhere dramatically different and unusual. This rocky world is covered in diamonds – and the sparkling sight is quite spectacular.

There's no life on Midnight – or so it is thought – but you can look out at the stunning landscape from the Leisure Palace. Life forms flock to this extravagant city to experience the height of luxury. It was lowered from orbit so that visitors are offered somewhere amazing to stay while enjoying the planet's many delights.

Midnight has lots to offer holidaymakers – whatever type of trip you are after. You can relax by the pool in the Leisure Palace Spa, or why not take a day trip to see some of the sights on the planet surface?

## ESSENTIAL INFORMATION

The planet has no air so don't be disappointed to discover you can't walk on Midnight's surface. Also the sunlight is X-tonic – and incredibly powerful. Luckily the glass in the Leisure Palace is thick enough to protect visitors.

## DAY TRIPS

While on Midnight, one of the highlights is a day out to the Waterfall Palace. Travelling across the planet in a secure Crusader vehicle, this four-hour trip is unforgettable – where else could you expect to see a sapphire waterfall?

## DID YOU KNOW?

When an enormous sapphire reaches the Cliffs of Oblivion it shatters to create a sparkling waterfall that tourists can watch from the safety of the Waterfall Palace.

## DON'T MISS

The antigravity restaurant (wear a bib!), the sapphire waterfall at the Waterfall Palace

## AVOID

Too much X-tonic sunlight (it burns), the planet's surface

# Who's Afraid of the Big, BAD WOLF?

From almost as soon as he met Rose Tyler, the Doctor was haunted by a phrase. Just two words. Bad Wolf. It took him a long time to realise they were significant, and even then he had no idea what the words meant. Was it a coincidence? Or a threat? Or was it some sort of message?

On Platform One, in *The End of the World*, the Moxx of Balhoon described the dire situation as a Bad Wolf scenario. But Rose and the Doctor were too busy trying to survive and save the spacestation from Lady Cassandra's plans to notice…

In *The Unquiet Dead*, Gwyneth – who is clairvoyant – was able to read Rose's mind. 'The things you've seen,' she said. 'The darkness… the big bad wolf…' Then, when Rose and the Doctor returned to Rose's home on the Powell Estate, a boy sprayed the words BAD WOLF on the TARDIS. The Doctor made him clean it off before they left on their next adventure. This took them a short way into the future – where Rose met a Dalek for the first time, and the unscrupulous collector Henry van Statten's helicopter call sign was Bad Wolf One.

Much further into the future, one of the television channels broadcast by Satellite Five was Bad Wolf TV.

And then in the past – when Rose tried to avert her father's death – Bad Wolf was once more graffitied across walls and posters.

Even Captain Jack had several Bad Wolf close encounters. The bomb that nearly killed him and blew up his spaceship in World War II had 'SCHLECHTER WOLF' painted on it – German for Bad Wolf.

In Cardiff, Jack helped the Doctor, Rose and Mickey avert disaster at the Blaidd Drwg project – and that's Welsh for Bad Wolf…

In the end it was not the Doctor, but Rose who realised what the words meant – and that it was a message. A message she had sent back to herself. A message that gave her the determination to get back to the Doctor and save him when she was trapped at home on Earth and all seemed lost.

She had been sent back home in the TARDIS from Satellite Five, now owned and run by the Bad Wolf Corporation. Seeing Bad Wolf graffiti everywhere around her, Rose realised that must mean she could get back to the spacestation. Spurred on by this, she opened the very heart of the TARDIS and looked inside. She saw the tremendous power of the Time Vortex itself, and she was possessed by it.

Rose was then able to use that power to defeat the Daleks, and to send the Bad Wolf messages back into her own time stream so that she gives herself the clue she has puzzled over. 'I am the Bad Wolf,' she realised. 'I create myself.'

Then she took the words Bad Wolf from the wall of the spacestation and scattered them back through time and space – 'A message to lead myself here.'

But if the Doctor and Rose thought that was the end of the Bad Wolf story, they were wrong. When they were forced to part company after defeating the Daleks and Cybermen and hurling them into the void between universes, the Doctor and Rose managed to meet one last time. The Doctor was able to project an image of himself through the last gap in the void before it closed. He met Rose on a beach in Norway. The place was called Dårlig ulv stranden –

But with the way between the universes closed, it seemed that the coincidence of Bad Wolf following the Doctor and Rose must surely now be ended. If only they had known the awful truth.

Because Rose Tyler was to return into the Doctor's life, and she brought with her a message. At first it was just a phrase – two words whispered to Donna to pass on to the Doctor. A message that meant nothing to Donna, but which would soon turn her life upside-down and prove more dangerous than any of her other perilous adventures with the Doctor.

Just two words.

# DEATH DISCO

... Here in the **Cosmos Ballroom**, the votes have been counted and verified!

The winners of **Universal Dance/Off** (nine million and two) are...

... From the planet Shivash, **Durrrin and Laliaargh!**

Bad luck to the Orthotrons, **Boris and Elsa!**

Clap

Clap

Clap

Clap

Fix! Fiiix!

... Where's that **independent adjudicator?** I'll give him something to verify!

Doctor, **do something!** Boris and Elsa, they've been robbed!

Donna, I can't take you anywhere...!

Hang on –

What's that **mirrorball** doing?

*Swoosh!*

*Fzzzak!!!*

Oh my-!

Durrrin and Laliaargh?

Eh? Where'd they **go?**

I dunno... but I'm **finding out!**

You coming?

# Destination: Earth

Earth has gone missing! Help the Doctor and Donna find it by following the migrant bees to find your way through the Tandocca Scale maze.

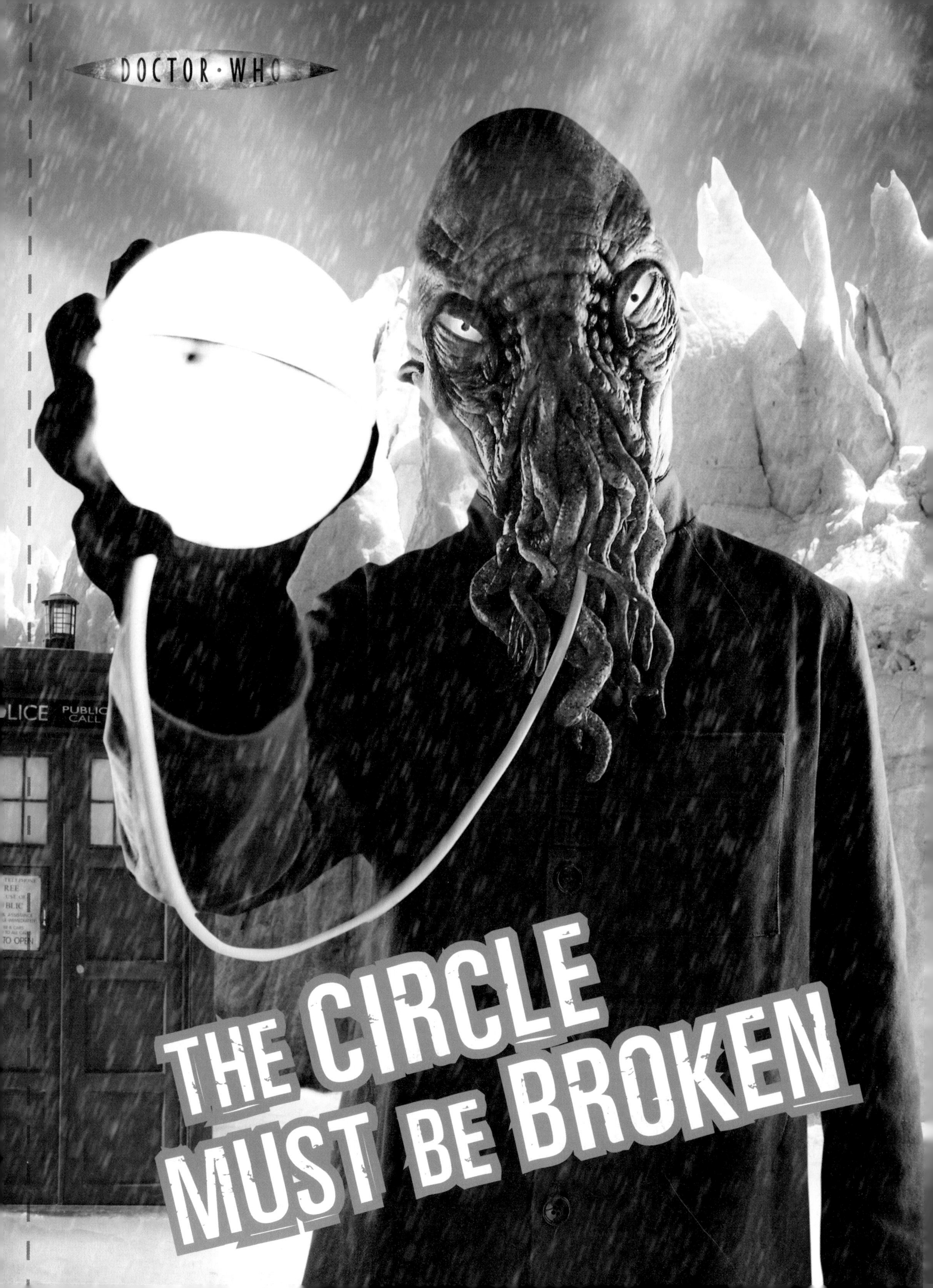

DOCTOR · WHO

THE CIRCLE
MUST BE BROKEN

# WHERE IN THE UNIVERSE ARE WE?

LOOK AT THE SETS OF CLUES BELOW AND SEE IF YOU CAN WORK OUT WHICH PLANET THE TARDIS HAS LANDED ON THIS TIME.

## A

You can see this in the night sky from Earth.

The Judoon took the hospital that Martha worked in there.

Some people say it's made of cheese!

## B

In the distant future, Catkind live there alongside humans.

The Face of Boe called the Doctor there to see him.

Both Rose and Martha have visited there with the Doctor.

## C

The Slitheen come from this planet.

It has a really long name and is quite hard to spell.

Its twin planet is Clom.

90

# What if...?

Have you ever wondered what might have happened if you'd done something differently? If you'd made a different choice, taken a different path, turned a different way?

For Donna, that possibility becomes real when she visits a strange fortune teller. Her life changes — her past changes. There was a moment when she made a decision, when she took a left turn in her car and went for a job interview that eventually led to her meeting the Doctor.

But the fortune teller asks her to imagine what would have happened if she had turned right instead. And it seems to happen, it seems to become real.

A small change, a tiny decision, but one with far-reaching and awful consequences. Because that small change meant that Donna never met the Doctor, and now the Doctor is dead. Without Donna's help, he died after defeating the Empress of the Racnoss.

And it's not just the Doctor. Without him it was up to Sarah Jane Smith to try to help the people in the Royal Hope Hospital when it was transported to the moon by the Judoon — and she died there, along with Martha Jones.

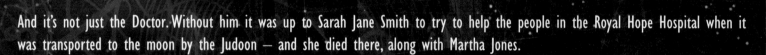

Without the Doctor, the Titanic crashed into London and destroyed it.

Donna was lucky to escape. Lucky to have met Rose Tyler who kept her safe, knowing that at some point history could be put back on track. But until then, Donna and her family are evacuated to Leeds where they share a crowded house with other refugees from the devastated London.

When Captain Jack Harkness and his Torchwood team die stopping the Sontaran invasion, there is no one left to defend Earth. And then the stars start to go out...

But Rose knows what's going on, and that Donna is the key. There's something on Donna's back, something that other people only glimpse. It's like a giant beetle that makes tiny changes to a person's life, their past. Only with Donna it created a whole new reality — a different history.

But the nightmare isn't over when history is put back on track. Donna's back with the Doctor, and everything's how it was. But she's got a message from Rose — and the Doctor knows the nightmare is only just beginning...

# Answers

## Page 14 Super Sonic

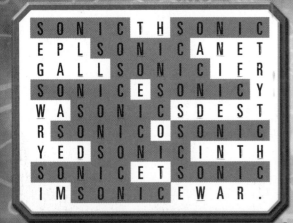

The message is: The planet Gallifrey was destroyed in the Time War.

## Page 26 Monster Mash

A and 3 are the Supreme Dalek.

B and 4 are a Hath.

C and 5 are an Ood.

D and 1 are a Sontaran.

E and 2 are Davros.

## Page 38 Trapped

## Page 40 Time Lord True or False

1 – True    2 – False    3 – True    4 – True

5 – False    6 – False    7 – False    8 – True

## Page 62 Cosmic Crossword

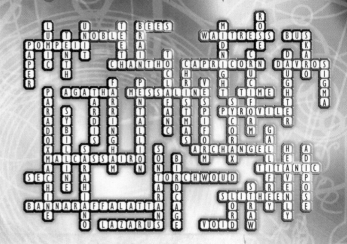

## Page 88 Destination: Earth

## Page 90 Where in the Universe are we?

A. The Moon.

B. New Earth.

C. Raxacoricofallapatorius.

# DOCTOR·WHO

## Available now:

DOCTOR·WHO
Model-Making Kit
POLICE PUBLIC CALL BOX
4 FANTASTIC MODELS TO MAKE

ISBN: 9781405902786
RRP: £9.99

TIME TRAVELS
DOCTOR·WHO

ISBN: 9781856130363
RRP: £17.99

## Available from October, 2008:

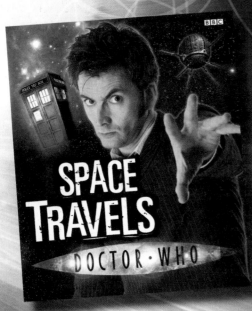

SPACE TRAVELS
DOCTOR·WHO

ISBN:9781405904285
RRP: £17.99

DOCTOR·WHO
DALEK
Pop-up Model Kit
GIANT DALEK
WITH PRESS-OUT AND MAKE PIECES

ISBN:9781405904261
RRP: £12.99

DOCTOR